LANA's WORLD

LET'S GO FISHING!

To Elliot, PK, and baby Daniel, with love
—E.S.

For Martha
—J.G.

Text copyright © 2015 by Erica Silverman
Cover and interior illustrations copyright © 2015 by Jess Golden

For information about permission to reproduce selections from this book,
write to Permissions, Houghton Mifflin Harcourt Publishing Company,
215 Park Avenue South, New York, New York 10003.

www.hmhco.com

The text of this book is set in Caecelia LT Std.
The display type was set in Gil Sans.
The illustrations were made with watercolors, pastels, and colored pencils.

Library of Congress Cataloging-in-Publication Data
Silverman, Erica.
Lana's world: let's go fishing / Erica Silverman.
p. cm. — (Lana's world) (Green light readers. Level 2)
Summary: Unable to interest her parents, her brothers, or even her dog in going
fishing with her, Lana creates her own boat and lake in her bedroom and soon
has all the company a girl could want.
ISBN 978-0-544-10652-9 paper over board
ISBN 978-0-544-10659-8 paperback
[1. Fishing—Fiction. 2. Family life—Fiction. 3. Imagination—Fiction.] I. Title.
PZ7.S58625Let 2014
[E]—dc23
2013004556

Manufactured in China
SCP 10 9 8 7 6 5 4 3 2 1

4500520604

LANA's WORLD

LET'S GO FISHING!

Written by **Erica Silverman**
Illustrated by **Jess Golden**

GREEN LIGHT READERS

HOUGHTON MIFFLIN HARCOURT
BOSTON NEW YORK

"Let's go fishing," said Lana.

"Not now," said Papa.

"I'm watching the game."

"Let's go fishing," said Lana.

"Not now," said Mama.
"I'm painting."

"Let's go fishing," said Lana.

"Boring," said Jay.

"Video games are more fun," said Ray.

"Let's go fishing," said Lana.

"Woof!"

Furry chased his tail.

"I will go fishing by myself," said Lana.

She went to her room.

She took out her fishing box.
She put little waves here
and big waves there.
She put blue fish here
and yellow fish there.
She put rainbow fish
everywhere.

She picked up her fishing pole.

"Now . . . let's go fishing,"
whispered Lana.

Her bed became a boat.

Waves rocked.

Fish flittered.

Lana rowed to the middle of the lake.

She sat, fishing by herself.

Papa peeked in.

"May I join you?" he asked.

"Swim out to the boat," said Lana.

Papa swam.

He picked up a fishing pole.

Lana and Papa sat fishing, side by side.

Mama peeked in.

"May I join you?" she asked.

"Swim over," said Lana.

Mama swam.

She picked up a fishing pole.
Lana, Papa, and Mama sat fishing,
side by side by side.

Jay and Ray peeked in.

"Fun," said Ray.

"Can we fish too?" asked Jay.

"Swim over," said Lana.

Ray and Jay swam.

They each picked up a fishing pole.

Lana, Papa, Mama, Jay, and Ray sat fishing,

side by side by side by side by side.

"It's so quiet,"
said Ray.
"I can hear the
water slosh
on the boat,"
said Mama.

"I can see the wind
ruffle the water,"
said Papa.

"Shhh," said Jay.

"You'll scare away the fish."

Furry poked his nose into the room.
"Woof!"

He ran—SPLASH!—into the water.

He jumped—THUD!—into the boat.

"Shhh!" everyone said.
Then they all laughed.
Lana hugged Furry.

"The best thing about fishing is that we are all together," she said.

Lana, Papa, Mama, Ray, Jay, and
Furry sat fishing, side by side by
side by side by side by side . . . until
it grew dark.

"It's time to go home," said Lana.
And she rowed the boat back to
shore.